Robert Munsch

Get Out Of Bed!

Illustrated by
Alan & Lea Daniel

Scholastic Canada Ltd.

Toronto New York London Auckland Sydney
Mexico City New Delhi Hong Kong Buenos Aires

This book was designed in QuarkXPress, with type set in 18 point Ellington Light.

Scholastic Canada Ltd.
604 King Street West, Toronto, Ontario M5V 1E1, Canada

Scholastic Inc.
557 Broadway, New York, NY 10012, USA

Scholastic Australia Pty Limited
PO Box 579, Gosford, NSW 2250, Australia

Scholastic New Zealand Limited
Private Bag 94407, Greenmount, Auckland, New Zealand

Scholastic Children's Books
Euston House, 24 Eversholt Street
London NW1 1DB, UK

Canadian Cataloguing in Publication Data
Munsch, Robert N., 1945-
Get out of bed!
ISBN 0-590-12473-0
I. Daniel, Alan, 1939- . II. Daniel, Lea. III. Title.
PS8576.U575G47 1998 jC813'.54 C97-932767-9
PZ7.M85Ge 1998

ISBN-10 0-590-12473-0 / ISBN-13 978-0-590-12473-7

For Amy Albrecht,
Tavistock, Ontario
–R.M.

To Carolyn and David
–A.D. and L.D.

In the middle of the night, when
everyone else was asleep, Amy went downstairs.
She watched
   The Late Show,
   The Late, Late Show,
   The Late, Late, Late Show,
   The Early, Early, Early, Early Show,
and finally went to bed because
she was feeling somewhat tired.

The next morning everyone came
to the breakfast table . . . except Amy.
   "Where is Amy?" said her father.
   "Where is Amy?" said her brother.
   "Amy is asleep," said her mother.
"I have called her five times and she is
still asleep. What are we going to do?"
   "No problem," said her brother.
"I can get her up."

Amy's brother ran up the stairs
and yelled as loudly
as he could: "**Aaaaaaammyyy!!!**"

Amy snored. **ZZZ-ZZZ-ZZZ-ZZZ-ZZZ-Z**

"Be late for school," he said. "See if I care."

And he ran back downstairs.

"Well, I know what to do," said Amy's father.

He walked up the stairs and said
in his sternest father voice, **"Amy, if you
don't get out of this bed this instant,
I am going to be very mad!"**

Amy snored. *ZZZ-ZZZ-ZZZ-ZZZ-ZZ*

He went back downstairs and told
Amy's mother, "YOUR daughter will not get up."

"Well, I have something that
sometimes works," she said.

She ran up the stairs,
stood Amy on her feet
and said very nicely,
"Amy, please wake up."

Amy fell over and
went to sleep on the floor.

ZZZ-ZZZ-ZZZ-ZZZ-ZZZ

Her mother ran back
downstairs and said,
"I can't get her up!
I can't get her up!"

"Oh no!" said her father.
"I have to go to work."

"Oh no!" said her brother.
"I have to go to school."

"I have to go to work, too,"
said her mother. "But what
are we going to do with Amy?"

"Let's take her to school in her bed,"
said her brother.

Amy's mother and father looked
at each other and said, "Good idea."

So they put Amy back in her bed and
picked it up. Then they walked
    out the front door,
    down the street,
    around the corner,
    through the schoolyard,
    and into the school.
They put the bed down in the back
of the classroom and left.

Later that day, the principal came in and said, "What is going on here?"

"I don't know," said the teacher. "It's Amy. She will not get out of bed."

"No problem," said the principal.

She walked over and yelled at Amy as loud as she could:

"**WAKE UP!**"

Amy snored. *zzz-zzz-zzz-zzz*

"I give up," said the principal.

So the teacher taught reading, and
Amy didn't wake up.
    The teacher taught arithmetic, and
Amy didn't wake up.

They went to gym, and Amy didn't wake up.

They went out for recess, and Amy didn't wake up.

They had lunch, and Amy didn't wake up.
They had art, and Amy still didn't wake up.

Finally, it was time to go home.

"Call the mother. Call the father," yelled the principal. "Get this kid out of here."

So Amy's mother came from work, and her father came from work, and her brother came from school. They picked up Amy's bed, carried it home, and all had dinner . . . except Amy. Amy was asleep.

ZZZ-ZZZ-ZZZ-ZZZ-ZZZ

"If she never gets up," said her brother, "can I have her room?"

But the next morning Amy did get up.
She ran downstairs and said, "Oh, I'm hungry.
I haven't eaten in years!"

"Nice to see you," said her mother.
"Did you have a nice sleep?"

"Wonderful," said Amy, "but I had
strange dreams."

Then her mother went to work and her
father went to work, and Amy and her brother
went to school.

At the door of the school,
the principal said, "Good morning,
Amy. How are you today?"

"Wonderful," said Amy.
"But I had strange dreams
last night."

"I bet," said the principal.

26

Then Amy walked
into her classroom and
everyone . . .

snored.

ZZZ-ZZZ-ZZZ-ZZ

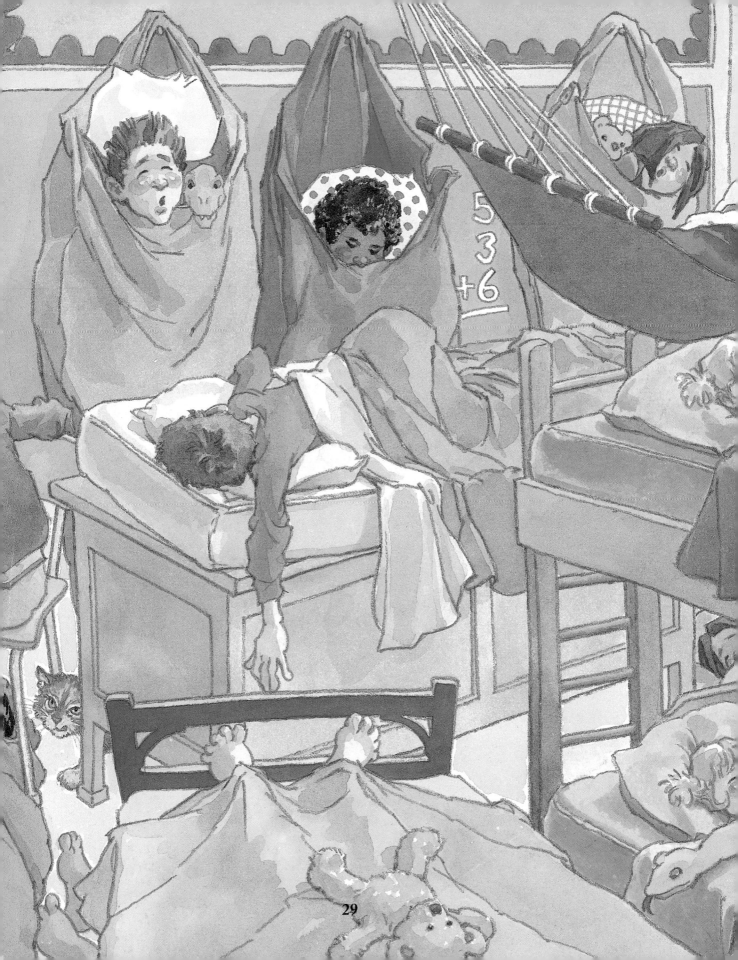